RESPECT

ReadZone Books Limited

© copyright in the text Marian Hoefnagel 2011
© copyright in this edition ReadZone Books 2017

Originally published in the Netherlands as *Doe normaal!*
© 2011 Uitgeverij Eenvoudig Communiceren, Amsterdam

Translation by Laura Dashwood

British Library Cataloguing in Publication Data (CIP) is available for this title.

All rights reserved. No part of this publication may be reproduced, stored in a retrieval system or transmitted, in any form or by any means, electronic, mechanical, photocopying, recording or otherwise, without the prior permission of ReadZone Books Limited.

ISBN 978-1-78322-629-0

Printed in Malta by Melita Press

Visit our website: www.readzonebooks.com

MARIAN HOEFNAGEL

RESPECT

Class 10B rallies against bullying

REALITY

Back to school

Kim and Peter walk into the school playground. It's the first day of school after the summer holidays.

'I wonder what our new form tutor will be like,' says Peter.

Kim nods. 'I hope it's a man,' she says.

Peter looks surprised. 'Why? What do you have against women?'

Kim grins. 'Nothing,' she says. 'But men come up with way more fun school trips.'

Peter shrugs. 'I don't believe that,' he says. 'That's got nothing to do with being a man or a woman.'

'You'll see,' says Kim.

There are already a lot of pupils in the assembly hall. Peter and Kim join their class. For the most part it's the same kids as last year. It was a nice class. Everyone thought so. The pupils and the teachers.

The head teacher steps on to the stage.

'Good morning, everyone,' he says.

He explains a few things about the new term. Four teachers have left. And four new ones have joined the staff. There was a mistake in the welcome letter sent home to Year 7 parents. Kim almost falls asleep.

Then the head teacher says, 'This is Mr Humphreys. He will be the new biology teacher and form tutor for 10B.'

'Hey, that's us!' Peter nudges Kim. 'Come on, we need to get to registration.'

Kim walks along with the other pupils of 10B. They follow Mr Humphreys.

'You got what you wanted,' says Peter. 'Our form tutor is a man. That's what you were hoping for, right?'

Kim looks at the new teacher. He's a bit chubby and walks clumsily ahead of them.

'That's the biology classroom, isn't it?' he asks. He points.

'No, it's over there,' says Jon. He points the other way.

Mr Humphreys looks around, surprised. Then he turns to the group of pupils. His eyes study them questioningly from behind his thick glasses.

'I don't really know my way around here yet,' he says shyly.

'Jon was just kidding,' Kim says quickly. 'You were right. It's this way.'

The new teacher

In the biology classroom, Mr Humphreys sits on his desk.

'You can call me Mr Humphreys,' he says. 'Or Sir, if you want. I will call all of you by your first names today. But if you prefer for me to call you Master or Miss, I can do that, too. You just have to let me know.'

The class laughs. What a funny idea: the teacher calling his pupils Master or Miss.

'I'm going to tell you something about myself,' he says. 'And it's not a jolly story. I don't tell it to every pupil. But you are my tutor group. I think you should know who I am.'

Mr Humphreys says it's his first day of school. And that he's quite nervous.

'I started teaching five years ago,' he says. 'At a school in a big city. There were difficult pupils at the school, I knew that. But I thought: I'll just try very hard. Then it will all be fine.' He takes off his glasses.

'I got on well with most of the pupils,' he continues. 'But with a few of them, I didn't. They started teasing. They called me rookie. I could laugh about that. It was true, of course. I was a rookie: someone who doesn't know anything about the job yet. Then they put a fake dog poo on my chair. I laughed about that as well.

'But the time after that, it was real poo. That wasn't a joke any more. And then they slashed the tyres of my car. And they rang me in the middle of the night. They shouted nasty things down the phone.

'They had no respect for me at all. Then one day they drowned my white mice in the aquarium. I'd brought them to school to teach about them. That really upset me.'

Mr Humphreys puts on his glasses again and looks around the class. All the pupils are listening very quietly.

'I got burnt out,' he says. 'I couldn't sleep. It took a very long time before I got better again. And when I was better, I didn't dare return to that school. But I did want to teach. That's what I studied for and what I like to do. A friend of mine works here, at this school. He said: "Come and work with us. I'll ask Mr Lee, the head teacher, if you can get the nicest classes to teach."'

Mr Humphreys stops for a minute. Then he says, 'So that means you should be the nicest tutor group here. I hope my friend was right. Because this is very exciting for me.'

A nice class

The class is sitting outside, in the playground.

'What do you think about Mr Humphreys?' asks Jamilla.

'I like him a lot,' says Kim. 'I think it's brave to tell us so much about himself.'

'But teachers never do things like that,' says Jon. 'I think it's a bit weird.'

Peter shakes his head. 'No,' he says. 'It's not weird, it's just... different.'

The others nod. Yes, that's what it is: different.

They continue talking about their PSHE assignment. Mr Humphreys doesn't like bullying. They can understand that. He's asked them to write about ways to stop bullying. How can you make sure you're not bullied?

'Talk to each other about it,' the teacher said. 'Discuss what you think is bullying. And what's just teasing.'

'I think it's tricky,' says Jamilla. 'I wear a headscarf. Boys often call me "Scarfy". I think it's annoying. But is it bullying?'

'If you don't like it, it's bullying,' says Peter.

'Yes, I think it's bullying,' Jamilla says. 'But I'm sure the boys who shout it at me don't think they're bullying me. They're just joking. It's different for everybody.'

'Not always,' says Jon. 'Drowning white mice isn't a joke.'

Yes, the others agree. Jon is right about that.

'We could make a contract,' Jon continues.

Huh? They look at him, surprised. Jon explains. 'The contract states that we won't bully each other. We won't bully any teachers either. And the teachers won't bully us. We'll all sign the contract together.'

Everybody nods. That seems like a good plan.

'But we'll need to work out what all of us think bullying is,' says Peter. 'Shouldn't that be in the contract as well? Like: you can't call Jamilla "Scarfy"?'

They all laugh.

'We'll ask Mr Humphreys,' Kim says. 'He knows a lot about bullying.'

Everybody laughs again.

Mr Humphreys is standing in front of the classroom window. He looks at his class, outside in the playground. It really is a nice class, he thinks. Luckily.

No ferry

Peter and Kim walk to the bus stop. They always travel home together. They live quite a long way from school. It's normally a forty-five minute bus ride. But today they have to take a ferry some of the way, too.

'I just hope we won't have to wait long for the ferry,' says Kim. 'Or I'll miss Hollyoaks.'
Peter laughs. 'That stupid soap,' he says. 'It doesn't make any sense. In one episode someone dies. And the next episode he's happily walking around again.'
'Aha!' Kim says. 'So you watch it too. Otherwise you wouldn't know that.'
Peter looks embarrassed. 'My sister watches it... so I've seen it once or twice,' he mumbles.
'Yeah, right. Soaps are addictive, you know. Once you start, you can't stop watching. Even my mum watches with me.'

Peter and Kim jump off the bus when it reaches the river. There's no sign of the ferry.

'What's that all about?' mumbles Kim. 'It was fine this morning.'

'Maybe it broke down,' says Peter. 'Goodbye, Hollyoaks,' Kim sighs.

More people arrive. They want to take the ferry as well. Everyone is disappointed that the ferry's not there. They look left and right. They peer into the distance.

'Nope, no There and Back,' sighs Kim.

Kim had laughed a lot when she saw the ferry for the first time. That was a few weeks ago. The new bridge was closed to be repaired. It was supposed to take six months, according to a big road sign. Cars and buses had to drive a long way over to the old bridge. But people on foot could take the ferry. The little boat was called 'There and Back'.

'That stupid boat drives me crazy,' says a man. 'One day it runs, the next it doesn't.'

'When we need to cross, it's usually here,' Peter says, surprised.

'Then I bet you only use it during rush hour,' the man says. 'They rented that boat for the school kids, like you. It runs before and after school. But any other time...'

The man shakes his head.

Waiting

'Here it comes!' shouts a girl. She's pointing into the distance. Kim stares in the same direction, but she doesn't see much.

'Do you see anything?' she asks Peter.

He nods. 'Yes... can't you see it?'

Kim shakes her head. 'My eyes are as bad as Mr Humphreys'.' she says. Peter looks at her.

'Your eyes are much prettier than his though,' he says. 'Your eyelashes are so long! I'd never noticed before.'

'They're a real nuisance,' Kim says. 'They're always bashing against my glasses.'

Kim blinks. Her lashes brush against the lenses. Peter laughs.

'I wonder why the ferry is coming from that direction,' Kim says.

'I don't know. But it'll take a while to get here,' says Peter. 'It's not exactly a racing boat, that There and Back.'

They sit next to each other on the grass. The weather is lovely and warm.

Suddenly having to wait around doesn't seem so bad.

'What are you planning to write about?' Peter asks.

Kim knows immediately what he means. The project about bullying.

'Some people get bullied because they have a weak spot,' Mr Humphreys had said. 'For example, my weak spot is my body. I'm fat, I'm clumsy and I have bad eyes. I could be bullied for any of those things. Have a think about what your weak spots are.'

'I'm fat and clumsy, too. And I have bad eyesight,' says Kim.

'What?' Peter looks at her indignantly. 'That's not true at all!'

'Yes it is,' says Kim. 'I never wear crop tops, or short skirts – why do you think that is?'

Peter looks at Kim. She's not super skinny, but she's not fat... No way!

'I can't do anything in P.E. Everyone always laughs at me,' Kim continues.

Peter nods. That is true.

'But you're a great swimmer,' he says.

'Yes, but now we're getting to the bad eyes,' says Kim. 'I love swimming. But I can't do that wearing glasses. And I can't wear contact lenses. They make my eyes red and sore. So I can't see what I'm doing or where I'm going in the pool.'

'I thought maybe you'd write about being adopted,' says Peter.

Kim looks at him, surprised. 'That's not my weak spot,' she says.

'It just seems a bit... weird... not to know your own mum and dad,' Peter says.

Kim thinks for a minute. Then she shakes her head.

'It doesn't bother me,' she says.

'What if someone teased you about being adopted?'

'I wouldn't care!' Kim replies, laughing. Then she jumps up.

'The There and Back's here!' she shouts.

Peter's weak spot

The There and Back is packed. Peter and Kim are the last ones to squeeze on to the small boat.

'We were the first ones here!' Kim mutters. The young ferryman smiles at her.

'Why did you go so far up the river?' Kim asks him.

'A dog fell off a big sand transport ship,' he replies. 'The captain didn't notice. I could see there weren't any passengers waiting for me at the time. So I rescued the dog and went after the sand transporter. Fortunately it was slow so I caught up with it.'

'Oh,' says Kim, 'I bet they were happy!'

The boy nods. 'Especially the dog,' he says.

They soon arrive at the other side.

'What are you going to write?' asks Kim as they ride on the second bus.

Peter stares into the distance. Should he tell Kim or not?

'I'm not sure yet,' he says, hesitantly.

'Do you have an idea?'

Peter nods. 'Yes, I have an idea. But, um... it's kind of difficult. I want to tell you all what my weak spot is, but... I'm afraid everyone will start picking on me. If they know.'

'Huh?' Kim says, confused.

Peter sighs. 'Okay, I'll tell you. I don't like it when they call me gay.'

'Oh,' says Kim. She thinks about it for a minute.

Yes, sometimes people call Peter gay, or sissy.

When he dyed his hair blond.

When he bought that cool leather jacket.

'But no one really means it, do they?' Kim says. 'It's just a joke.'

'Well, that's the point.'

Again, Kim doesn't understand.

'What do you mean?' she asks.

Peter sighs. He looks at Kim.

'They're right,' he says. 'I don't fancy girls. I like boys.'

Kim almost falls off her seat in shock.

'You're not serious!' she gasps.

'Yes,' says Peter, 'Yes, I am'.

Poor Kim

Kim is sitting in front of the TV with a cup of tea. *Hollyoaks* is on. She looks at the screen, but doesn't really see anything. She thinks about Peter and what he told her.

'Well,' says her mum, 'That Amy is up to something.'

Kim is startled. 'What?'

Her mother points at the television. A pretty blonde girl is sneaking around.

Kim laughs. 'She's up to something!' she says.

'Yes, I just said that,' says Kim's mum. 'Your thoughts aren't really with *Hollyoaks*, are they?'

'No,' Kim sighs.

Her homework isn't going smoothly either. Kim's can't help thinking about Peter all the time. It was silly of her not to realise. They've been taking the bus to and from school together for two years now.

They often do homework together and test each other. Sometimes they go to a movie, or a school disco together.

Of course, everyone at school thinks Peter and Kim are dating.

Peter always laughs whenever anyone asks if they're a couple.

And he always just says, 'Kim's very special.'

Now she understands why.

She always thought Peter was shy. That he didn't dare to ask Kim out. But of course he was never in love with her. She's just a friend. A bus friend. A homework friend. A dancing friend. But not his girlfriend.

Kim sighs. Just my luck, she thinks. I fall in love, but it's with a gay boy. Poor me.

She lies down on her bed. She wishes it would swallow her up. But it doesn't, of course.

Poor me, she thinks again. Poor pathetic me.

Poor Peter

'Hey, sleepyhead.' Kim's mother pokes her head around the door. Kim wakes up with a start.

'We're going to have dinner in a minute,' says her mum.

Kim sits up straight. 'I fell asleep,' she says, surprised.

'I can see that!' Kim's mum laughs.

Kim isn't feeling very hungry.

'What's the matter with you?' her dad asks. 'Spaghetti's your favourite. Have you fallen in love or something?'

Kim sticks her tongue out at him. 'I always fall in love with the wrong men!' she sighs.

Everyone laughs.

'You sound like a woman in her thirties,' her dad says. 'Not like a fifteen-year-old girl.'

'Still, it's true,' says Kim. 'I used to want to marry you. That was wrong, wasn't it? Then I fell in love with my Year 5 teacher. That didn't end well. And now...'

They all look at Kim expectantly.

Kim takes a deep breath. 'The boy I'm in love with is gay.'

Kim's parents look at each other, surprised. Her little sister nearly chokes on her spaghetti.

'Peter?' her mum asks softly.

Kim nods.

'I thought so,' says her mum.

'What? That I was in love with him, or that he's gay?'

'Both,' her mum says. 'Poor Peter.'

'What do you mean, "poor Peter"?' says Kim crossly. 'You mean, "poor Kim"!'

But Kim's mother shakes her head. 'You'll fall in love with someone else one day,' she says. 'But Peter's going to have a hard time. It's not easy for a guy to come out. His parents might not like it. Other boys might tease him about it. Girls will be disappointed. It's not going to be easy for him. He didn't ask to be gay, Kim. It's just how he is. And he's going to have to live with it.'

'Okay. Poor Kim and poor Peter, then,' says Kim.

Angry

The next morning Kim doesn't wait for Peter. She takes the bus to the ferry. But she's out of luck – the ferry is on the other side of the river. She has to wait until the There and Back gets over to her side again.

'Hiya,' she says to the ferryman. 'Save any more dogs today?'

The boy laughs and shakes his head. 'I'm saving you instead.'

'How so?' asks Kim.

'If I wasn't here to take you across, you'd be late for school.'

Yes, that's true. Kim jumps on to the little boat.

The guy is just about to leave when Peter arrives at the little port on another bus.

'Wait!' shouts Peter. 'Wait for me!'

Hurrying, he steps on to the ferry.

'Why didn't you wait for me?' he asks Kim. 'You always wait for me!'

Kim shrugs. 'Just because.'

Peter looks at her, surprised, but he doesn't say anything.

'Have a nice day!' the ferryman says when they reach the other side.
'You too!' says Kim, stepping off the ferry.
Together with Peter, she is about to climb on to the next bus.
But Peter won't let it go.
'We need to talk,' he says. 'This is more important than being on time for school.'

Kim sighs. If only Peter had gotten angry. Then she could have lashed out. But Peter is very calm.
'Let's have a drink,' he says.

Cutting class

They sit in the window of the café by the canal. They can see the There and Back across the water. Peter has ordered them both a hot chocolate. It tastes good.

'And now you're going to tell me what's wrong,' he says.

Kim stares out of the window. She doesn't want to look at Peter.

Of course it wasn't very nice of her to leave him behind. They wait for each other by the park every morning. And now, for the first time in two years, she had left without him.

'Is it because of what I told you?' Peter asks. Kim nods.

'I really didn't expect this sort of thing from you,' Peter says, sadly.

Kim suddenly feels sorry for him.

'You don't understand,' she says. 'I don't care whether anyone's gay or not. But I do care about you. I, um...' She stares into her empty mug.

'I just hoped that you felt the same way about me... as I do about you,' she says softly.

Peter looks relieved. 'Oh, thank goodness,' he says.

'What!' says Kim indignantly.

Peter takes her hand. 'Sorry,' he says. 'If I liked girls, Kim, I'd choose you – really! I think you're the most amazing girl in the world.'

'That doesn't help a bit,' says Kim. But it does make her smile.

'I'm afraid to tell people I'm gay,' says Peter. 'I'm afraid they'll suddenly look at me differently. I'm scared they won't like me any more. But I'll have to tell everyone some day. My parents. My friends.'

'Your parents don't know yet?' asks Kim, surprised.

'No,' says Peter. 'You're the first person I've told.'

Kim flushes with pride. 'Oh right... I see,' she says.

'I wanted to talk to you first. I thought: Kim's my best friend. If I can't tell her, I can't tell anyone.'

Kim nods. 'I'm sorry for leaving you,' she says. 'I was only thinking about myself. But this is harder for you. I see that now.'

Peter looks at her gratefully. 'It's a real shame, Kim. It would have... you know... been easy to fall in love with you.'

'Shouldn't you two be in school?' asks the owner. 'It's nine o'clock!'

'We're on our way,' says Kim.

They get up and head off to school.

A good contract

Mr Humphreys looks surprised when Kim and Peter walk into the classroom. They're very late; the PSHE lesson is almost over.

'Did the ferry break down?' he asks.

Peter shakes his head. 'We needed to talk,' he says.

'Oh,' says Mr Humphreys, and he doesn't ask any more questions. Then the bell rings.

'Next time it's Kim and Peter's turn!' Mr Humphreys shouts over the noise. 'They will have to sign the contract. Remember to respect each other in the meantime!'

The class shuffles out into the corridor.

At break the others tell Kim and Peter what they missed in class. Jon had written the anti-bullying contract. It was very short. Some people thought it was too short. They wanted it to be longer. The class had discussed it. Then they made the contract longer. And better. Everyone who signs the contract has to tell the class something about bullying.

Jamilla told them that she doesn't like to be called Scarfy. But that this might not be bullying. Mr Humphreys had thought about that for a minute.

Then Jon had said, 'Sweet Scarfy isn't as bad as Stupid Scarfy.'

The whole class laughed, but Mr Humphreys took it seriously.

'That's a very good point, Jon,' he said. 'It's about the intention behind the words. Not necessarily the words themselves.'

'We need to take the contract to the other Year 10 groups,' says Jon, 'Everyone should sign it. The teachers, too.'

'Let's just try it with our own class first,' mutters Peter, 'I think that's difficult enough.'

But Jon doesn't want to listen. 'It's such a good idea!' he says. 'We should tell the Department of Education.'

Everyone laughs. Crazy Jon. He always goes over the top with everything. Then the bell rings again, and they have to go back inside.

'What are you going to do?' Kim asks as they

walk to their next class.

'What do you mean?' asks Peter.

'Will you tell the class what you told me?'

'I'm not sure yet,' replies Peter. 'But I will if I'm brave enough'.

'I'll support you,' Kim promises.

Class without a teacher

But the next day, Mr Humphreys isn't there at registration.

'He's ill,' Mr Lee explains.

'When will he be back?' asks Kim.

'I don't know,' the head teacher says. 'Mr Jones will be taking his classes today.' He nods at the supply teacher and leaves the classroom.

At the end of the day, the class has a free study period.

'I hope Mr Humphreys didn't get burnt out again,' says Jamilla.

'I don't think so,' Peter says. 'He's not being bullied here, is he?'

'Maybe he got nasty phone calls again,' says Kim. 'From his last school. Maybe he can't sleep again.'

Peter shrugs. 'Maybe he broke his leg,' he says.

'I'll ask Mr Lee!' says Jon.

Everyone thinks that's a good idea.

When Jon gets to Mr White's office, his

secretary is on the phone. 'Hold on a moment,' she says to the caller. Then she turns to Jon. 'Can I help you?'

'I just want to know what's wrong with Mr Humphreys,' says Jon.

'Oh,' says the secretary. 'Well I'm speaking to Mr Humphreys right now. Would you like a word?'

Jon takes the phone. 'Hello?'

'Yes, hello, this is Mr Humphreys.' His voice sounds strange.

'Oh,' Jon says. 'You've got a cold.'

Mr Humphreys laughs. His laugh immediately turns into a coughing fit.

'No it's hay fever,' he says. 'I've got a very bad pollen allergy. Look it up. You'll learn something.'

'Okay,' says Jon. 'We'll wait to do anything with the contract until you get better.'

'Good,' says Mr Humphreys. 'I'll try my best to be back at school soon.'

'Great!' Jon says. 'We've got big plans for the contract. But we'll tell you when you get back.

Get well soon, Mr Humphreys. From all of us.'

Back at the classroom, Jon says, 'We need to look up hay fever. Mr Humphreys is allergic to pollen.'

'I saw something about that in our biology book,' says Jamilla. 'It was somewhere near the back.'

A few moments later they're all hard at work.
Kim writes "Pollen = dust" on the board in neat writing. When the head teacher walks into the class, he is surprised.

'I thought I'd better check on you... as Mr Humphreys isn't here to supervise your study period. What are you working on?' he asks.

'We're studying biology,' Jamilla explains.
'Very good,' mutters Mr Lee. 'I'll leave you to it then. He nods and walks out again.

At the end of the hour, there's a lots of information about hay fever on the whiteboard. A lesson made by 10B.

Short and fat

'What's your new form tutor like, then?' asks Kim's mother.

'Nice,' says Kim, her mouth full of food. 'But he's off sick right now.'

She walks across the room holding a sandwich. She takes another bite whilst heading for the sofa. She plops down. The cat wakes up with a start and leaps off the sofa. Kim jumps and drops half the sandwich. The cat quickly walks over to it. It's a tuna sandwich. He likes tuna. He bites into the sandwich and runs away with it.

'Stupid cat,' mutters Kim. 'Thief.'

'I think that was fair enough,' says Kim's mum. 'You gave poor Pear a fright. He took revenge.'

Kim looks at the cat called Pear. He's sitting on the windowsill, eating. Pear really does look like a pear.

He is a strange shape for a cat. He has a small head and a very fat body.

'That sandwich will make you even fatter,' Kim says to Pear. 'And it serves you right. Stealing it from me. Bully.'

Kim's mother laughs. Then Kim laughs, too.

'Oh well,' she says. 'If Pear eats it, then it won't make me fat'.

Kim's mum shakes her head. 'You're not fat,' she says.

'Yes I am,' says Kim. 'Almost all the girls in my class are skinnier, except for Justine. Justine's just as fat as I am. But that's because she's ill.'

'Justine is a lot bigger than you are, love,' says Kim's mother. 'You should be happy with who you are. You look great.'

'I'm too short,' Kim says. 'Short and fat.'

Kim's mother sighs. 'I'll tell you again,' she says. 'All Colombian girls are much shorter than British girls. And perhaps a bit more shapely, too. That's just how it is. You were born there. Your mum was probably short, too. The funny thing is, you're pretty tall for a

Colombian girl.'

'But short for a British one,' Kim mutters. 'And fat.'

'I give up,' says her mother. 'I'm going to make myself a tuna sandwich.'

'Make me another half too, please!' shouts Kim.

A welcome return

'How long does hay fever last?' Jamilla asks. 'It doesn't say in the biology book.'

Mr Humphreys isn't at school again today. The notes on hay fever are still up on the whiteboard.

Just then the head teacher walks in.

'It looks as if you lot had a really good study session yesterday,' he says.

The class nods and points at the board. Mr Lee reads the information on it. When he's finished he turns to the class.

'I think it's great,' he says. 'Now I understand exactly what's wrong with Mr Humphreys, as well.'

'When will Mr Humphreys be feeling better?' Jon asks.

'That's hard to say,' says Mr Lee. 'But I'm surprised you don't know that... after all your research.'

Jamilla says, 'But we didn't find that out.'

'As long as there is pollen in the air, it will make Mr Humphreys ill,' says the head teacher. 'But he's taking medicine for it, so hopefully it won't be long.'

A few days later, Mr Humphreys is back at school. The class is excited that he is back. They spend the whole of registration talking to him about hay fever, and what they learnt about it.

When the bell rings, Mr Humphreys says, 'Tomorrow we'll carry on with our bullying contract in PSHE.'

Kim looks at Peter. It's their turn next time. Mr Humphreys said so. Next time they have to sign the contract. And talk to everyone about their weaknesses. Peter smiles at Kim. He knows what she's thinking.

'What a nice photograph,' says Jamilla. She's pointing at a picture on Mr Humphreys' desk of a woman. A young woman.

'That's my wife,' Mr Humphreys says. 'Or at least, she used to be.'

'Used to be?' asks Jamilla.

'Yes,' Mr Humphreys sighs. 'I'll tell you about her another time.'

Peter's still Peter

The next day they have their PSHE lesson with Mr Humphreys. They're all very quiet because he is telling them about his wife.

'She couldn't handle the bullying,' he says. 'Those horrible phone calls just kept coming. We changed our phone number, and it was quiet for a while. But then the phone calls started up again. She got scared. And I couldn't reassure her. One day my car was badly scratched. The next there was dog poo left on our doorstep. In the end, she went to stay with her parents.'

'But she can come back now, can't she?' asks Jamilla. 'Everything's all right now, isn't it?'

But Mr Humphreys shakes his head.

'She thinks it's me. She says I'll always be a target for bullies. When I was at school myself, it was even worse. Children used to push me in the lake because I was fat. "You'll float!" they said. They used to lock me in the greenhouse because I was allergic to the pollen.

"Let's see if you sneeze", they said. I told my wife all of that. So she's too afraid to live here with me now. She's afraid I'll keep getting bullied. And that if we ever have children, it will happen to them, too.'

The class is deathly quiet. Nobody knows what to say.

'Yes,' Mr Humphreys sighs. 'Bullying can get very bad. And it always starts with a joke.'

'I have to sign the contract,' Peter suddenly says. 'I'll tell you about my weakness. About my fear of being bullied.'

Peter looks at Kim for a moment. She nods her head. Then Peter comes straight out with it. He's gay. He doesn't mind. But he's been afraid to share it.

'So far I've only told Kim,' Peter says. 'And now, you guys. I hope you won't bully me for it. You've called me sissy and stuff before. I know it was meant as a joke. But it wasn't nice.'

Again, the class is silent. They're learning a lot today. There's a lot to think about.

Jon is the first person to speak.

'How does Kim feel about it?'

Kim blushes. 'Makes no difference to me. Peter's still Peter,' she says. 'I respect him just the same.'

Happy about yourself

Everyone in the class has signed the contract. And everyone's said something about their weak spot. They know a lot of things about each other now. And that feels really good.

Most things they could have guessed. Justine isn't happy with her weight. She told them it's because of an illness. Not because she eats too much.

Robin hates the fact that he can't live with his parents. He lives with his old grandmother. She's sweet, but she's ill a lot. Robin has to take care of her. His gran should really be in a nursing home. But then Robin wouldn't have anywhere to live.

Jon thought for a very long time. 'I'm happy with myself,' he said.
The class laughed. Yes, they can understand that. Jon's parents are rich. Jon gets everything he wants.

He just got a top-of-the-range bike for his fifteenth birthday. He's got an expensive mobile phone. He wears designer clothes. And he's good-looking, too: tall and blond.

'I respect that,' Mr Humphreys had said. 'But still... even you must have a weak spot. Give it a bit more thought, Jon.'

Kim told them that she's adopted, but she doesn't mind.

'What bothers me is that I'm too short and too fat,' said Kim. 'And I've got bad eyesight. And I'm always a joke in P.E., because I'm clumsy. I wish I was more like Leah. She's so tall and slim. And so flexible.'

But Leah didn't agree with her at all. 'I'm too skinny!' she had said. 'And have you seen my feet? They're a size 8. I look like Tweety. And my hair looks like rope. I wish I had Kim's hair. And Kim's feet.'

'It's not easy to be happy with yourself as you are,' Mr Humphreys says at the end of the lesson. 'But you should always try to respect yourself and others. Some things can be helped. Bad eyesight, for example, can be corrected nowadays. Hopefully a cure will be found for Justine's disease. But these big feet of yours, Leah... Well, you'll just have to get used to big shoes.'

The class laughs.

A surprise

A few weeks later, Mr Humphreys makes an announcement.

'So... we're going on a survival trip. A few days away.'

Mr Humphreys looks at the class expectantly.

The class has got a lot of questions. How long will they be away for? Where will they sleep? Will they go by bus? Are they the only ones or will there be other kids going?

Mr Humphreys' eyes twinkle at them from behind his glasses. He knew they would be excited.

Most Year 10 classes just have a day trip this term. To a theme park, or something. Year 11 pupils at the school always go away for a week. To Paris or Amsterdam or Prague. They can choose. Classmates never all choose the same city. And Mr Humphreys thinks that's a shame.

He's looking forward to a trip with his whole class.

'Why did you organise this, Mr Humphreys?' Jon looks at him, questioningly.

'Well,' says Mr Humphreys, 'I'm not sure if I should tell you that'.

The class settles down immediately. Mr Humphreys always tells them everything. Or almost everything.

And now he won't tell them why he organised this survival trip?

But Mr Humphreys laughs, 'I'm kidding.'

Then he's serious again.

'The anti-bullying contract is a big success,' Mr Humphreys says. 'I showed it to the other teachers at a staff meeting. Everyone loves it. All the teachers are going to use it in their classes now. Mr Lee thought you deserved a treat, as a reward for all of your hard work. So I suggested this trip.'

Mr Humphreys takes off his thick glasses and cleans them.

Kim wonders if he is crying. But she can't tell.

'That's cool, Mr Humphreys,' says Jon, 'I wish

all teachers were like you.'

'That would be a bit exhausting, with all these trips to organise,' says Mr Humphreys.

The class laughs.

All taken care of

'Do you think the trip is going to be expensive?' Robin says it quietly, but everyone hears him.

Mr Humphreys nods his head. 'It's not cheap, but we're going to earn the money ourselves,' he says. 'We're going to work together on Wednesday mornings.'

Everyone starts shouting again.

'Does that mean we don't have school?'

'How can a whole class work somewhere?'

'What are we going to do? How much will we earn?'

'Calm down,' says Mr Humphreys, 'If you listen, I'll explain everything.'

And then he begins.

Every Wednesday, they'll have to get up early. They'll start work at seven o'clock. One group will stock shelves at the supermarket close to the school. Another group will work in the nursing home, cleaning and preparing food for the people there.

A third group will work at the post office, sorting and delivering post. A fourth group will work in the swimming pool, cleaning and helping out with swimming lessons.

'I want to work at the post office,' says Jon.
'And I want to help with swimming lessons,' says Kim.
'No, that's not how it works,' Mr Humphreys says. 'The groups will change. Everyone will go to the post office at some point. And the nursing home. And the supermarket. And the swimming pool. You'll dislike some of the chores and like others. That's just how it works. But...'

Mr Humphreys looks at them mysteriously.
'I was able to make sure that this work is counted as work experience. You all have to do work experience this year. Usually you have to find a placement for yourselves. You'd work in a shop or an office for a week and write a report on it. And then you'd get a grade.
'For you lot it will be different,' he continues.

'You won't have to find your own placement. Of course, work experience is usually unpaid. But this time, the employers have all agreed to make a contribution to the trip... if you do a good job! So, we'll work together to raise the money. And the best thing is that everyone will be able to go. Your parents won't have to pay for anything.'

The pupils beam at Mr Humphreys. He really has thought of everything.

Jon's weak spot

'Any questions?' asks Mr Humphreys.

Jamilla puts up her hand. She looks sad.

'My parents won't let me sleep over anywhere on my own,' she says.

Mr Humphreys nods. 'Is there anyone else who has to sleep at home, or who want to?'

Hesitantly, Jon puts up his hand.

Everybody looks at him, surprised. But Mr Humphreys doesn't ask any questions. 'All right,' he says. 'The camp isn't far away. So, I'll make sure you're brought home every night. And every morning someone will pick you up. Okay?'

Jamilla and Jon nod happily.

'I, um… I'll tell you why, if you like,' says Jon.

'Go ahead,' Mr Humphreys says.

'I get really bad homesickness,' explains Jon. 'I've had it for as long as I can remember. I could never stay over at friends' houses. Or at my grandma's. I tried a few times. But, in the end, my dad always had to come and pick me up. In the middle of the night. I really hate it. Especially now. It sounds so cool to go camping with all of you. But I... I just can't.'

'I'm glad you've told us,' says Mr Humphreys. 'And... now we know your weak spot.'
Jon looks sad.
'It's really embarrassing,' he says. 'I wish I could get over it.'
'That's often the case with weak spots,' says Mr Humphreys.

'Why didn't you say anything before?' asks Kim, frowning.
Jon looks at her questioningly.
'When you signed the contract,' Kim says.
Again, Jon looks sad.
'I just feel really silly about it. I thought, no one needed to know.'

'That's not fair,' Kim says. 'We all talked about our weak spots. You should have, too.'
'You're right,' says Jon. 'But I thought you'd

take the mickey out of me.'

'What was that contract about, again?' Mr Humphreys asks.

Jon nods, ashamed.

Robin

Jon and Robin are sitting on the benches in the school playground. They're talking about the trip.

'It sounds amazing,' says Robin. 'Survival – it sounds so exciting.'

Jon nods. It sounds good to him, too. But it's nicer for Robin. He's never been away on a holiday before.

'What will you do about your gran when you're away?' asks Jon.

Robin looks very sad for a minute. What will he do?

'Maybe I can cook some meals and leave them ready for her to warm up,' he says. 'Or ask the neighbours for help. We'll see.'

Peter and Kim head off to the bus stop. 'See you tomorrow,' they call out to Jon and Robin.

'Yeah, I've got to go, too,' says Robin.

Jon gets on his bike. Robin stares at it, feeling jealous. It's such a great bike.

'Do you want a ride?' asks Jon.

But Robin shakes his head. 'There's someone waiting for me,' he says, and he walks off.

On the way home, Robin is lost in thought.
He hopes his gran won't get ill while he's on his school trip. Because then he'd have to go home. And that would be a shame. Mr Humphreys' plan is amazing. No one has to pay for anything.
I bet he thought of that for me, thinks Robin.
The work sounds good, too. The swimming pool, the post office, the supermarket. All fun. The nursing home sounds boring, though. Looking after one old person is more than enough for him.

Robin is soon home. He climbs the concrete steps at the block of flats.
It's a shame there's no lift here, he thinks. *That would be a lot easier for gran.*
He's so lost in his thoughts, he almost bumps into his neighbour.
'Sorry,' he says to the woman. 'I was miles away. I was thinking these steps are so steep.

And how hard it is for gran to walk up and down them.'

The neighbour nods. 'It's not easy for older people,' she agrees.

Working in a swimsuit

Mr Humphreys has made a schedule to divide up all the jobs. Kim and Jamilla are going to the swimming pool next Wednesday. Some of the other pupils are working there, too.

'Do I have to wear a swimming costume?' asks Jamilla. She and Kim are sitting on the little wall in front of the school at break time. Mr Humphreys is standing next to them.

'I don't know,' says Mr Humphreys. 'It depends on what kind of work they want you to do.'

'I'll take my swimsuit,' says Kim. 'Maybe they'll let me help with the swimming lessons. That sounds so cool.'

'It sounds good to me, too,' says Jamilla. 'But I don't think my dad will like it.'

Kim hadn't thought of that. And neither had Mr Humphreys.

'You can tell the people at the swimming pool that, can't you?' asks Kim.

'What should I say?' asks Jamilla.

'That you can't work in a swimsuit,' Kim says. She laughs. It sounds so weird.

'I could secretly bring my swimming costume,' says Jamilla, 'And not tell my dad.'

But Mr Humphreys shakes his head.

'No,' he says. 'It's not a good idea to lie to your parents, Jamilla. And if your dad found out, you might not be allowed to come on the school trip with us. That's what we're doing all of this for, after all.'

Yes, that's true.

'I'll give the swimming pool a ring,' says Mr Humphreys. 'If you don't want to tell them yourself. But I think you should. You'll learn something.'

Jamilla nods, but she doesn't look happy.

'I'll be there with you, too,' says Kim. 'We'll tell them together. It's always easier when you're not alone.'

Jamilla smiles at Kim. 'That would be great,' she says.

'We could go to the swimming pool today after school,' says Kim.

'Yes, that's a good idea,' Mr Humphreys says. He takes out his diary and leafs through it.

'Here, I have it,' he says. 'You should ask for the pool manager, Mr Waters.'

Kim and Jamilla burst into giggles.

'That can't be true!' Kim shouts.

'It is,' says Mr Humphreys. 'But remember: you must be respectful. You're not to laugh about his name. He can't help what he's called. I think he gets plenty of comments about it already.'

The first day of work

'Well, how did it go?' Mr Humphreys looks around the classroom expectantly. It's Wednesday. They had all been to work that morning.

Everyone starts shouting out. Mr Humphreys can't understand a thing. But it all sounds enthusiastic.

'One at a time!' Mr Humphreys shouts. 'First, the group at the swimming pool.'

Kim says that she helped with the swimming lessons. Jamilla and some of the others helped in the canteen. They had to make tea and coffee and do the washing up.

'Did you have fun?' Mr Humphreys asks. The pupils nod. It was a lot of fun.

'And Peter?' asks Mr Humphreys. He had been to the post office with Jon.

'We had fun, too,' says Peter.

'It was tiring, though,' says Jon. 'They sent us out on a mail round. And we had to hurry to get back here in time.'

'Couldn't you go on your bike?' asks Mr Humphreys.

'I asked them,' says Jon. 'But it wasn't allowed.'

The group that worked in the supermarket is happy as well.

'Stacking shelves is boring,' says Robin. 'But we got to do it in pairs and hang out a bit. And now I know exactly what kinds of coffee there are. And how much they cost.'

'Is it hard work?' asks Mr Humphreys.

'It's okay,' says Robin.

Justine tells them about the nursing home.

'Everything's very calm and peaceful there,' she says. 'I like that. And the old people are very sweet. And so happy that we were there to help them.'

One of the boys tells them about an old lady who used to be a singer. She was quite famous.

'She thinks she still is,' Justine grins. 'She goes down the corridors with her walking frame, singing.'

'So it's all a success?' Mr Humphreys asks. The class nod as the bell rings.

'Great, well off you go to class,' says Mr Humphreys.

Posters

'We're going to work on your reports,' says Mr Humphreys. Reports? The class look at him in surprise. Which reports?

'Did you forget?' asks Mr Humphreys. 'You have to write a work experience report. All Year 10 pupils have to do it. I told you.'

They remember now. They have to write about their work. In the supermarket. In the swimming pool. In the post office. In the nursing home.

'Do we need to write four reports – one for each place?' asks Jon. 'That's a bit much.'

'No. We're going to do things differently,' says Mr Humphreys. 'In fact, we're going to make four posters. We'll split the class into four groups. Every group makes one poster. You can decide which group you want to be in.

'Every poster should have pictures and text. And a title. For example: "The Swimming Pool Is For Everyone". Then you write something about the swimming pool. Why it's so good for you to go swimming. How nice the swimming pool is. What sort of jobs you can do there. That sort of stuff.'

It's a nice idea. They start making plans immediately.

Jon joins the swimming-pool group. 'My dad has a good camera,' he says. 'I'll take care of the photographs. And I'll take Leah with me as a model.'

'Make sure her big feet aren't in the picture!' Robin says. He surprises himself. Was that bullying?

But everyone laughs. Including Leah.

'Plan your design first. Then you can use the computers to help make your poster,' says Mr Humphreys. 'That way, you can type up the text and use coloured backgrounds. You can print out pictures, too. Mrs Smith in the IT suite will help you after school.'

The groups are formed. They all get to work. Soon, the bell rings.

'Hey,' says Jon to his group. 'That was quick. Shall we work on it after school? We can meet up at my place later.'

It's a good idea. The rest of the swimming-pool group nods.

A plan

They're sitting in Jon's room. Jon's mother brought them tea and biscuits. Jon has a big bedroom, with a beautiful balcony. But they can't sit out on it now. It's too cold and they should be working. Working on the poster for the swimming pool. But they're talking. About Mr Humphreys.

'I'm enjoying school much more this year,' says Kim. 'It's really thanks to Mr Humphreys.'
The others agree with her.
'We have to do something for him,' says Peter. But what?
'What would Mr Humphreys want most of all?' asks Jamilla.
They all think for a moment.
'That there's no bullying,' says Robin.
'That his wife would come back to him,' says Kim.
They all fall silent.
'How are we going to make that happen?' asks Peter. 'We don't even know his wife's name.'

'Sina,' says Jamilla, 'His wife's name is Sina.'

They look at Jamilla, surprised. How does she know that?

Jamilla grins. 'It's written on the photo, on Mr Humphreys' desk.'

'Do you know her last name, too?' asks Jon.

But Jamilla shakes her head. That wasn't on the photo.

'Maybe we can ask Mr Humphreys if he talks about her again,' says Kim. 'But we mustn't let him know our plan.'

'What will we do, when we find out her name?' Peter looks at the others questioningly.

Kim hesitates. 'Maybe we can write her a letter. We could say that Mr Humphreys told us about her. We can ask if she wants to talk to him again.'

But Peter doesn't like that idea.

'Why don't we ask her to come on our school trip with us,' says Jon. 'We'll make up an excuse.'

Peter thinks that's a much better idea.

'We could do that,' he says. 'But we need to know her surname first. And her address.'

'Yes,' says Kim. 'But for now we should really get to work on this poster.'

They sit down at the table. Kim and Jamilla start writing the text. Peter and Jon look for images on the computer. Robin reads the leaflet from the swimming pool.

Another plan

Going to work on Wednesday mornings is normal, now. In two weeks, they will be finished. That will be strange. Nice, of course, that they won't have to get up so early. They made enough money to pay for the school trip. It's getting closer and closer now. They're going in only two months.

They've made lists of stuff that they need to take. And it's quite a lot: warm clothes, solid boots, raincoats... you can never be sure of the British weather. But they're hoping it will be nice: warm and sunny. Then the survival won't be so tough.

The posters are almost finished. They've worked hard on them. Mr Humphreys has called a parent-teacher meeting tomorrow night.

'The posters should be up in the classroom by then,' he says. 'Your parents will like that.'

Everything is going fine. They just need to find Mr Humphreys' wife.

They still don't know what her last name is. Or where she lives. They can't just ask Mr Humphreys. And he's never mentioned his wife spontaneously again.

They've searched for Sina Humphreys in the phonebook. It was possible she still had Mr Humphreys' last name. They phoned all the S. Humphreys. At Jon's house. They laughed a lot. But they didn't find the right S. Humphreys.

'She probably doesn't use the surname Humphreys any more,' says Jon's mother one afternoon. 'Or perhaps she never did.'

They're working on the poster for the swimming pool again. The text and photographs need to be stuck on. Jon took some great shots of Leah at the pool. They match the text perfectly. The group hopes they will help them to get a high grade.

'Sina could be short for something,' says Jon's mum. 'Maybe her name is Josephina.'

'I guess Sina won't be coming with us,'

Jon says, disappointed.

But his mother thinks they shouldn't give up so soon.

'I have a little plan,' she says.

'What kind of plan?' asks Jon.

'I'm not telling you,' his mum says mysteriously.

'Well then, why bother saying anything,' Jon mutters.

The parent-teacher meeting

There are a lot of parents in Mr Humphreys' classroom. They're looking at the posters that are displayed on the walls. Mr Humphreys has put a big pot of coffee on his desk, and a plate of biscuits. Kim's mother made a cake. It's next to the coffee.

'Are we having a birthday party?' jokes Jamilla's father.

Jon's mother is still in the hall. She's talking to Kim's mum.

'Are you coming inside?' asks Mr Humphreys. 'Then we can begin.'

The mothers walk into the classroom, giggling. Mr Humphreys tells the parents about the school trip. About everything the pupils are going to do. And everything they still need to arrange.

'Jamilla and Jon need to be picked up in the evenings,' says Mr Humphreys. 'And brought back in the mornings. Is there anyone who can help with that?'

Jon's mother can bring them; Jamilla's father can pick them up.

Then Mr Humphreys tells them about Robin's grandmother. He asks if anyone can stop by to see her while Robin's away. All the mothers put up their hands.

Mr Humphreys laughs. 'That might be a bit too much for her,' he says. 'One visitor is enough. Who lives nearest to her?'

That's Jamilla's mum. She will check in on Robin's gran every day.

'I can cook for her, too,' she says.

Mr Humphreys rubs his hands. Things are going well. The parents are drinking coffee and chatting to each other.

'Mr Humphreys, come and join us,' says Jon's mother. Mr Humphreys sits down next to her.

'Jon told me about your wife,' she says. 'Her name is Sina? That's a very special name. I used to have a best friend named Sina. I'm wondering if it could be the same person. What's her last name?'

'Rose,' says Mr Humphreys.

Jon's mother shakes her head.

'No, my friend's last name was Nicholas,' she says.

'I know a Rose family!' Kim's mother says. 'They're from Cambridge. Is your wife from Cambridge?'

'No, she's from Bath,' says Mr Humphreys.

'Oh,' says Kim's mother. She looks disappointed.

An article in the newspaper

Kim roars with laughter when her mother tells her about the parent-teacher meeting.

'It is a bit mean,' says Kim's mum. 'Poor Mr Humphreys didn't suspect a thing, but it's for a good cause.'

Kim agrees with that. And so do the others. Jon and Kim are very proud of their mothers.

Now they can work on a plan. But it isn't easy. How can they get Sina to come with them on their trip? What kind of excuse can they give?

Later, the group meets up at Jon's house. His mother walks in with a newspaper.

'Look!' she says. 'You could do something with this.'

'What are we going to do with a stupid newspaper,' mutters Jon.

'There's an article in here about Mr Humphreys,' she says. 'Kim's mum and I wrote it. About the anti-bullying contract. And how much of a success it is. The head teacher said so himself. There's much less bullying at the school now. And it's all thanks to Mr Humphreys.'

Jon and Kim grab the newspaper.

'That's so cool!' shouts Kim. 'What an amazing idea!'

'We'll send this to Sina!' says Jamilla. 'Then she'll see how amazing Mr Humphreys is.'

'And there's a picture of Mr Humphreys in it,' says Robin.

'I took that at the parent-teacher meeting,' Jon's mum says with a grin.

In the photo, Mr Humphreys is standing in front of the posters. Underneath the photograph it says:

Mr Humphreys is the new teacher of class 10B. The pupils say he is their favourite teacher ever.

'Well,' says Jon's mum, 'I'll leave the rest up to you. Kim's mum and I have done enough. I'll make you another pot of tea. And that's it'.

'Could you bring some biscuits, too?' asks Jon, 'or would that be too much?'

'Way too much,' says his mum. But she brings the biscuits anyway.

'We'll write Sina a letter,' says Robin. 'And we'll send her the newspaper article'.

'What will we write in the letter?' asks Peter. 'We haven't decided on our excuse yet.'

'Maybe we should just tell her the truth,' says Jamilla.

They all look at her in surprise.

The letter

Dear Sina,

We hope you don't think it rude of us to call you that. But we don't know whether to call you Ms Rose, or Mrs Humphreys. We're not sure if you're still Mr Humphreys' wife or not.

We're the pupils of 10B, the class Mr Humphreys teaches. As you can see from the newspaper article, Mr Humphreys is a great teacher. We've learnt a lot from him. Especially about bullying. And how bad it can get. He told us how he was bullied himself. And how awful it was. About how he couldn't sleep. And how he lost you, his wife. We found it very shocking.

So we made an anti-bullying contract. Everyone at our school uses it now. It's really helpful.

Because it's such a success, the head teacher is going to let us go on a school trip for a few days. Mr Humphreys arranged it for us.

We're going on a camping and survival trip on 5th June. It'll be very cool.

Anyway, here's our question. We would like to give Mr Humphreys something to say thank you. And we think the thing he would like most would be to see you again. Would you join us as a supervisor? Mr Humphreys will sleep in a big tent with all the boys and one of our mums will sleep in the girls' tent. She knows we're writing this letter to you and she thinks it's a great plan. She'd be happy for you to join us.

We really hope you'll come. It would be so nice for Mr Humphreys. He doesn't know anything about this, of course!

Kind regards from all of class 10B

At the end of the letter, they all sign their names. They fold the letter and put it in an envelope with the newspaper article. They write Sina's address in Bath on it. Now they just need a stamp.

The letter drops into the postbox. They're a little nervous. What will Sina think? They hope she writes back soon.

What now?

But Sina doesn't write back.

'Should we call her?' asks Kim.

'Maybe she just doesn't want to come,' says Peter.

'Maybe she didn't get the letter,' says Kim.

'I'm a bit scared about ringing her,' says Jamilla. 'But I think we should.'

They're huddled together in the school playground. In one week's time, they're going on the trip. Everything's been taken care of, except for Sina.

'What sad faces!' Mr Humphreys says, walking towards them. 'We're going camping together! Aren't you excited?'

They try to smile. But unfortunately, it doesn't really work.

'Are you worried about your mock exams next month?' asks Mr Humphreys.

They nod. They can't exactly tell him what's really going on.

'We'll draw sticks,' says Kim when Mr Humphreys has gone. 'One will be shorter than the others. I'll hold them so no one can see which is the shortest. We all have to choose a stick. Then the person who draws the short one has to phone Sina.'

They all nod. They understand.

Kim goes over to a nearby tree. A little later she walks back. She's holding some sticks in her hand. They all draw one. No one pulls the short stick.

Kim sighs. 'I guess that means it's me then. I'll phone her later this afternoon, when I'm at home. I don't want to do it when you're all listening.'

'Do you want me to ring Sina?' asks Peter, as they head home together. Kim looks at him. *That's sweet*, she thinks.

'No, we drew sticks fair and square,' she says.

'Good luck with it, then. See you tomorrow.' Peter turns the corner.

'Yeah, see you tomorrow,' says Kim.

The camp

Excited, class 10B stands next to the bus. There are rucksacks, suitcases, kids and parents all over the pavement.

'Aren't we ready yet?' someone shouts.

'No, Mr Humphreys isn't here,' someone else replies.

Mr Humphreys isn't here? Where could he be? They can't leave without him. Then the head teacher arrives.

'You can get on the bus,' Mr Lee says. 'Mr Humphreys is driving there in his own car. He just rang me. He'll meet you all at the camp. Leah's mother, Mrs Harris, will supervise you.' He nods at Leah's mum who smiles back.

'That's a bit weird,' Jon mutters. They've worked towards this all year. And now Mr Humphreys is going in his own car.

It's cosy on the bus. The driver has switched on the radio. They sing along with the latest pop songs. Luckily there's no traffic.

One hour later, they arrive at the camp. The bus drives into the grounds, and there's Mr Humphreys.

The plan with Sina didn't work out. Kim rang the phone number in Bath. A Rose family did live there. But Sina didn't.

'Hello, Mr Humphreys! Was the bus too cramped for you?' They get off the bus, laughing.
'I decided it would be best to have a car with me,' Mr Humphreys says. 'What if someone gets ill? I'd need to get them to a doctor quickly.'

The kids drag their bags over to the large sleeping tents – one for boys, one for girls. They make their beds with mats and sleeping bags. They're soon done. Camping is easy. Then they head to the food tent.
Mr Humphreys divides them into groups. One group has to prepare the food today. The other groups will take it in turns to do it in the coming days.

Survival

Mr Humphreys tells his pupils what they're going to be doing. They're going to cycle. They're going to go jogging. They're going to make rafts and sail on them. They're going to go swimming. And hang off ropes above the water. They're going to build a bridge with branches and run across it. They'll crawl through tunnels. They'll climb trees. They'll find their way back to the camp in the dark, with a torch.

It all sounds fun. But Kim's afraid she'll be laughed at. She's good at swimming, but hanging off ropes...

'Now remember, it's important to respect each other. We know that everyone has strengths and weaknesses.' The pupils smile.

'We'll work in teams,' says Mr Humphreys. 'Everyone has to do everything, but only the three fastest times in each team will be counted.'

Thank goodness, Kim thinks. *Then I can*

take my time. And I don't have to worry about falling off the ropes.

'We'll start this afternoon, after lunch,' says Mr Humphreys. 'The group preparing the food will stay here. The other teams will build rafts and go cycling. And this evening we'll all go for a hike with our torches.'

Kim is in the group that will be making the food. She walks to a corner of the food tent. There is the stuff for lunch. Together with the others, she starts making sandwiches. Leah's mother helps them.

'Tonight we're having spaghetti bolognese,' says Leah's mum. 'It's easy, so it won't take long to make.'

'Do we have to do the washing up as well?' asks Kim.

'Yes,' says Leah's mother. 'I think so'.

'I'll help you with that,' a voice says.

Surprised, they turn around. A pretty young woman is standing in the tent.

Kim recognises her immediately. 'You're

Sina!' she shouts. 'You came!'

Sina nods.

'Does Mr Humphreys know I'm coming?' she asks.

'No,' says Kim. 'We haven't told him anything at all. But didn't you see him? He was just outside.'

Sina shakes her head. No, she hasn't seen Mr Humphreys.

'I don't understand,' says Kim. 'We couldn't find you. How can you be here?'

Sina laughs. 'That's a long story,' she says.

The food group

They finish preparing the food quickly. There is soon a big pile of sandwiches in the food tent.

'We can call everyone in,' says Leah's mother. She walks outside. She's wearing boots, because it's raining a little. Kim notices that Leah's mother has big feet too.

Then Kim spots Sina's backpack on the floor. 'Why don't I show you where to put your stuff?' she says.

'That would be great,' smiles Sina.

When they're in the girls' tent, Kim asks, 'What will you do now? Are you joining us for lunch?'

Sina hesitates. 'I don't know. What do you think I should do?'

Suddenly, Kim has an idea.

Tonight they're going to walk in the woods, with their torches. Mr Humphreys said they had to look for some treasure. Well, Kim's going to make sure that treasure is found. By Mr Humphreys!

'Stay here,' Kim tells Sina. 'I'll bring you some sandwiches. I'll tell you my plan in a minute. When the others are here.'

Kim goes back to the food tent. At first she thought it was a shame that she had to prepare the food for this afternoon. But now she doesn't mind at all.

After lunch, the groups get started. One group is going cycling. Mr Humphreys rented mountain bikes. They're at the entrance of the camp. It's still raining a bit. That's a shame. But tomorrow the weather will be better, Mr Humphreys says.

The other group is going to build rafts. There are a lot of branches at the lake. And rope. They can't use any nails. Mr Humphreys will help them with the rafts. The P.E. teacher joins the cycling group.

The food group is busy washing up. It's a lot of work. Luckily, Leah's mother and Sina help them.

When the dishes are done, they sit down at the table together.

'Let's start on the spaghetti bolognese,' says Leah's mum.

They cut onions, clean carrots, wash leeks, and put the tomatoes in hot water. Everyone has a task. While they're cooking, Kim says, 'Now I want to know what happened. Tell us, Sina! Did you get our letter after all?'

Sina's story

And Sina tells them. She got 10B's letter with the newspaper article. She had been very surprised, but very happy as well. She was so pleased to hear that everything was going well for Mr Humphreys, but she didn't know what to do. She was glad that 10B had invited her. And she liked the idea of seeing Mr Humphreys again.

But what if Mr Humphreys didn't want to see her? The class said he did, but how could they know for sure?

Then she'd thought: "I'll go to visit my best friend in London."

She wanted to talk to her friend about Mr Humphreys and about the letter from 10B. "She'll know what to do," Sina had thought.

It was while Sina was in London that Kim had phoned. Sina's dad didn't know about the letter. He just thought about the nasty phone calls Sina used to get. So he'd told Kim that Sina didn't live there.

When Sina got back from London, she'd told her father about the letter. Then he had understood.

Sina had decided to go to the camp. Her friend had said, 'Of course Mr Humphreys will like it if you go. He told his class about you. He'll think it's amazing if you show up. They'll need people to help out. Maybe he won't be in love with you any more. But still, a camp will be fun regardless. And who knows what will happen when you two see each other again...'

But by that time it had been too late to write back. And Sina didn't have Kim's phone number, or anyone else's in the class.

'Oh, how silly,' Kim says. 'We forgot to write that in the letter.'

'So I thought I'd just come along to the camp,' Sina says. 'I knew you were arriving today. And... that's the story.'

Kim takes a deep breath. Now she needs to tell them her plan.

'Are you guys still working?' Leah's mother asks. 'Come on, peel those tomatoes, cut those carrots, grate some cheese, wash the lettuce. I'll put the mince on to fry. This isn't just time for a chat, you know!'

Kim's plan

The food group is sitting together. Let the others go mountain biking and rafting. They're making plans for tonight. Exciting plans.

'We'll set the tables,' says Kim. 'We'll prepare everything and then we'll go and sit in the girls' tent. We can make our plans there. Mr Humphreys won't disturb us.'

The mountain bike group returns, exhausted. It was tiring because the paths were very muddy. But it was cool! The girls lie down on their sleeping bags. Then the raft builders return. They, too, enter the tent.

'We have something to tell you,' Kim says. 'Someone special has come to join us.'

By dinner time, everybody knows about Sina. Except Mr Humphreys. And everyone knows about Kim's plan. It's a very good plan. During dinner, there's a lot of whispering going on. And a lot of laughing. But luckily, Mr Humphreys doesn't notice a thing.

When it's almost dark, Mr Humphreys says: 'Listen, everyone. I'm going to give you a map, with a marked route on it. You have to search for the treasure. It will be at the cross. We'll go in groups of four. Each group will have a torch and a compass. The first group will leave now, the next group will leave five minutes later, and so on. It's about time to start. The first group to find the treasure wins it. But watch out: there's danger along the way!'

Laughing, the groups head off into the dark forest. Mr Humphreys is the last person to leave. He heads straight for the treasure. He's carrying a few emergency flares. If a group takes too long, he can light one. Then pupils that are lost can walk towards the light. Yes, Mr Humphreys has thought of everything. Well, except for one thing.

It's very dark in the woods. They hadn't expected that. They can't see much, even with the torch. It's cloudy, so there's no moonlight, and there are no stars.

In the city you can always see something on a dark night like this. But not in the woods. There are no street lights here.

Scary

It's not easy, finding the right way. All the trees look alike. And strange things happen in the woods. Sometimes they see something white running between the trees. Or are they imagining it? Then they think they see a large animal. Or maybe not? They hear strange sounds. It sounds like soft crying.

Peter's group was the first to leave. Peter shines some light on the compass with the torch.

'We should be heading in the right direction,' he says. 'It's that way.'

Peter is speaking very quietly. He's not sure why. But it's pretty scary being in these dark woods at night.

Suddenly they stop. The strange sound is very close by now.

'What should we do?' Jamilla asks. 'Should we check it out, or just carry on?'

'Let's go and see what it is,' Peter whispers.

He walks cautiously into the bushes.

There, behind that tree, that's where the sound is coming from. It sounds like a little girl crying.

'What if it's a ghost!' Jamilla is spooked. 'I'm scared.'

'Ghosts aren't real,' Peter says, firmly.

'That's what you think,' mutters Jamilla. 'I'm staying here. You go and look.'

Peter looks nervously behind the tree. He doesn't see anything. He shines the torch on to the ground. Still, he sees nothing, only leaves. He takes a deep breath and moves the leaves with his hands. And then... he laughs.

'Come and have a look at this ghost,' he says.

The rest of the group comes over for a look. On the ground is an old cassette player.

'Mr Humphreys!' groans Jamilla. 'Just wait. He's about to get a shock himself.'

Jon's in the next group. He doesn't feel safe in the woods. He would rather be riding his bike through the city. The woods are too quiet.

And he keeps thinking he's seen something. But then it's gone. There, between those trees, isn't that a big, scary animal?

Jon points. The others think they see something, too. But what is it? There aren't really any dangerous animals in the British countryside, are there? It couldn't be a bear, could it?

Then the large animal moves. They scream. Jon drops the torch. When he picks it up again, he shines its light at the animal. But there's nothing to see.

A flare

The trek through the forest seems to last all night. But really they've only been searching for an hour and a half. Still, Mr Humphreys is starting to worry. Somebody should have found the treasure by now. If one group was late, he would have understood. But nobody has arrived yet. And the route wasn't that difficult, was it? *Should I light a flare?* Mr Humphreys thinks. But it's still a little early for that.

In the meantime, Kim's group have stopped in their tracks. They see a woman floating in between the trees.

'That's not possible,' Kim whispers, 'There's no such thing as ghosts.'

Still, they all see it. Slowly, the woman floats from tree to tree. She's wearing a long, white dress. They can't see her head properly. Or her feet. Then, suddenly, she's gone.

'Let's take a closer look,' says Kim.

Bravely, she heads over to where the woman was floating. She shines the light of her torch on to the ground. It's muddy, from the rain. There are footprints in the mud. Big footprints, from wellies.

Then Kim laughs. Suddenly, she understands.

'That was Leah's mum,' she laughs, 'She was wearing big boots today.'

The others laugh now, too.

'Mr Humphreys, we're going to get you,' says Kim softly.

Mr Humphreys is really starting to worry now. What could have happened?

It's getting very cold. *What if the kids get sick*, Mr Humphreys thinks. *It would be my fault.* He gets a flare out of the plastic bag and lights it. With a sizzle, the rocket shoots up. A big red ball comes out of it. The ball lights up the entire area. A spooky red light. It's quite pretty.

The whole forest should be lit now, Mr Humphreys thinks. He looks around to see if he can spot anyone. And...

Mr Humphreys thinks he must be dreaming. There, in between the trees, is Sina. She looks like a fairy. She's wearing white clothes that look pink in the light.

A fairy tale

Slowly, Sina walks over to Mr Humphreys. He takes off his glasses and rubs his eyes. He's got to be dreaming. How can Sina be here? Mr Humphreys puts his glasses back on and looks again. Sina's still there. And she's not alone.

The pupils of 10B slowly emerge into the clearing.

It's a magical sight with all that red light. It looks like something from a fairy tale. But then the red ball of light fades away. The flare is used up. Mr Humphreys can see less and less, until it's completely dark.

But now the torches are switching on. And the pupils start to talk.

'You didn't expect that, did you, Mr Humphreys?'

'You thought you could give us a fright, didn't you?'

But Mr Humphreys doesn't hear the cheerful pupils.

He looks at Sina, who's still walking towards him. She smiles at him.

'Is it okay if I join your survival trip?' she asks.

Mr Humphreys doesn't know what to say. He just nods.

And then more figures emerge from the woods. Leah's mother, wearing boots and a white dress. The P.E. teacher in a bear costume. Jamilla's father with the cassette player. They all laugh.

'So where's the treasure?' asks Leah.

'It's standing right in front of me,' Mr Humphreys says, earnestly.

Sina laughs. 'It was your class's idea,' she says.

'Yeah,' says Peter, 'You made this year so great, Mr Humphreys. We wanted to do something special in return. So we came up with Sina.'

'I don't know what to say,' says Mr Humphreys.

'But where's the treasure?' Leah asks again.

'Start digging,' Mr Humphreys says. 'Treasures are always buried.'

They look around. Dig? Where?

'There are shovels over there!' Jon shouts.

'And there's a cross on the ground here,' says Kim. It makes her laugh.

Two white blankets are draped on the ground in the shape of a cross.

Soon they're all digging.

The end of the trip

The school playground is packed. But not with pupils. There are only parents. Parents of the pupils in 10B. They're waiting for their children. They are getting back from their survival trip today.

Robin's grandmother is waiting as well. She came with Jamilla's parents in their car. Jamilla's mum enjoyed taking care of Robin's grandma. She said: 'My own parents live so far away. Spending time with Robin's grandmother is like having a mother in this country.'

Robin's grandma likes Jamilla's mother very much, too. She came over every day to chat and bring her food. Robin's grandmother had never tried Moroccan food before. But she thinks it's delicious.

'I'll still come and visit and bring you food when Robin is back,' Jamilla's mother says. 'That'll make life easier for Robin as well.'

Robin's grandma smiles at her and nods. 'That would be lovely.'

There's the bus.
'They won't have crawled under the seats, will they?' says Kim's mother.
The other parents laugh. No, they're too old for that. They did do it a year ago. But not now, surely.
The bus stops in front of the school gates. No pupils get off. And no one can be seen in the windows. Huh? The parents look at each other.
'Surprise!' the class jumps up by the windows. Laughing, they roll out of the bus.
'You should have seen your faces!' Kim shouts.
Kim's mum shakes her head, laughing.

Mr Lee, the head teacher, is there, too.
'And, did Mr Humphreys survive?'
They all look at him happily and point towards the end of the street.
Mr Humphreys' car has just appeared there. Sina's behind the wheel. She pops her head out of the window.

'My husband was too tired to drive,' she says. 'He's sleeping.'

It's true. Mr Humphreys is asleep in the back seat.

'And,' Kim asks Peter. 'Was I right, or not?'

Peter looks at her, surprised. 'About what?' he asks.

'About male teachers coming up with the best ideas for school trips,' Kim says, laughing.